Wallpaper from Space

by Daniel Pinkwater
illustrated by Jill Pinkwater

Atheneum Books for Young Readers

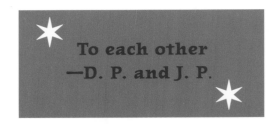

To each other
—D. P. and J. P.

Atheneum Books for Young Readers
An imprint of Simon & Schuster Children's Publishing Division
1230 Avenue of the Americas
New York, New York 10020

Book design by Ethan Trask
The text for this book is set in Cheltenham 18 pt.
The illustrations are rendered in pen, ink, and colored markers.
Printed in Singapore

First Edition
10 9 8 7 6 5 4 3 2 1

Library of Congress Cataloging-in-Publication Data
Pinkwater, Daniel Manus.
Wallpaper from space / by Daniel Pinkwater;
illustrated by Jill Pinkwater.—1st ed.
p.   cm.
Summary: At bedtime, a young boy enters the outer space-
patterned wallpaper in his room and has adventures with a band of spacemice.
ISBN 0-689-80764-3
[1. Outer space—Fiction. 2. Adventure and adventurers—Fiction.
3. Humorous stories.] I. Pinkwater, Jill, ill. II. Title.
PZ7.P6335Wal   1996
[Fic]—dc20
95-36393

Contents

Changes

Steve's mother was redecorating. Steve was very confused. She had decided to change the whole house around. She got rid of Steve's table and chair, and forgot to ask him if he wanted to keep the little stool in the bathroom that turned into a ladder when he brushed his teeth. Steve knew he didn't need a ladder anymore, but still, Steve thought, she could have asked.

Steve sat at the table in the kitchen and stared at the wall. Nothing was the same. Steve's mother came in and out of the house carrying things. She had new paint for the living room walls, and wallpaper with flowers all over it for the bathroom.

Steve's mother piled all the things for changing the house on the floor. She looked at Steve. She could see something was wrong.

"Steve?" she asked.

"Steve went away," Steve said.

"Who is that sitting at the table?"

"Nobody."

"Nobody looks very sad. Does nobody know why?"

Steve couldn't stand it any more. "Everything is changing," he howled.

  5

Steve's mother sat down beside him. "You know, I've been thinking. Maybe you'd like to have some new wallpaper in your room."

Steve stared out the window. "No."

"Are you sure? I saw some very nice wallpaper in the wallpaper store today. It had racing cars on it."

"Yech," Steve said.

"They had wallpaper with cowboys."

"Ick. I'm going to throw up."

"Horses?"

"Nope."

"If you could have any kind of wallpaper in the world, what would it be?"

"Lions," Steve said. "Lions eating people."

"I'm pretty sure they don't have wallpaper with lions eating people," his mother said. "What would be your second choice?"

"Crocodiles eating people."

"They don't have that either."

"Cannibals eating people?"

"Steve, they just don't make wallpaper with people getting eaten. It isn't a popular idea. In the wallpaper store, right beside the racing car wallpaper was some spaceship wallpaper."

"Spaceships?"

"It was really nice."

  6

Steve's mother had trapped him. He sort of wanted to see the spaceship wallpaper. His friend Brian had spaceships on the lining of his sleeping bag, but even Brian didn't have spaceships on his bedroom walls.

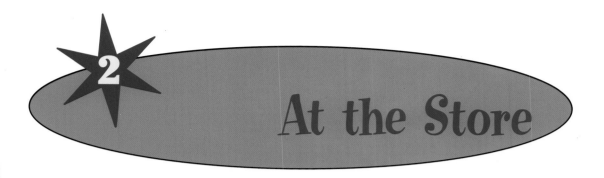

At the Store

They drove to the wallpaper store.

"Do the spaceships on the wallpaper glow in the dark?" he asked his mother.

"I don't know," his mother said. "They might."

The wallpaper store was big. It smelled like the art room at school. It was sort of a neat place. The spaceship wallpaper was the wallpaper of his dreams. It was deep space blue and the spaceships were real interstellar vehicles. There were even little spacemen floating around, spacewalking. If Steve squinted he could almost see the spaceships flying across the wallpaper, having space wars.

"Wow!" Steve said. "Do these spaceships glow in the dark?" he asked the wallpaper man.

"Yes, they do," the wallpaper man said.

"What do you think?" his mother asked him.

"I think redecorating is neat!" Steve said.

On the Wall

"When can we put this up in my room?" Steve asked his mother on the way home in the car.

"How about tomorrow?"

After breakfast, Steve helped his mother put up the wallpaper. He was a big help. She said so.

They didn't finish until after lunch. The room looked different.

"It looks like space," Steve said.

Steve's mother got up on a ladder. With a brush she painted white stars all over the ceiling.

"You can hardly see them!" Steve said.

"Of course you can't see them," Steve's mother said. "You know you can't see stars in the daytime."

"How about at night?" Steve asked.

"Wait and see."

When it got dark, Steve and Steve's mother and Steve's father all crowded into Steve's room and turned the lights off.

It was fantastic.

"This is fantastic!" Steve's father said.

"Isn't this fantastic?" Steve's mother said.

"Ooooh!" Steve said.

"This is really fantastic," Steve's father said.

"It's really fantastic, isn't it?" Steve's mother said.

"Ooooh!" Steve said.

"Boy," Steve's father said. "This is some fantastic room."

"It really is sort of fantastic, isn't it?" Steve's mother said.

"It sure is a fantastic room," Steve's father said.

"Well, how do you like your room?" Steve's mother and father asked him.

"It's fantastic," Steve said.

Steve could hardly wait to go to bed. He lay in bed looking at the wallpaper and the stars his mother had painted on the ceiling. He felt as if he were floating in space. The spaceships seemed to zoom across the sky. The spacemen tumbled and turned in space.

Then he made a big discovery. There were dark places between some of the spaceships. The dark places were round and swirling. Steve knew what they were. They were black holes. They sucked things up and spit them out at the other end—sometimes into whole new worlds.

This worried Steve. He was scared for the little spacemen floating around the spaceships. "Look out!" Steve yelled. The spacemen were getting too close to the black holes. Steve waved his arms and kicked his legs. When he did that, he began to spin and turn. He rose up off his bed. There were stars all around him, and spaceships. Some of the spacemen were waving to him.

"Look out for the black hole!" Steve shouted.

He heard a tiny voice, like a mouse's voice, far away. "Which one?"

"That one! That one there!" Steve shouted. "It's a black hole!"

"Don't worry about it!" the spaceman shouted in his mouse's voice. Steve realized that his voice sounded like a mouse's voice too. He shouted back to the spaceman, "What do you mean, don't worry about it? It's a black hole! It can suck you up!"

"Don't get excited," the spaceman shouted. "We'll throw you a rope."

Steve saw something coming toward him, curling and looping. The spaceman had thrown him a rope.

"Tie that around your middle," the spaceman shouted, "and we'll pull you in."

Steve tied the rope around his middle. He felt the rope

tug. He was moving through space. The spacemen were pulling him in.

He was getting closer to a spaceship. It got bigger and bigger. "Oh, boy! This is neat!" Steve thought.

A door opened in the spaceship's side. Steve floated through the door. It closed behind him.

Meeting the Spacemen

Steve looked around at the inside of the spaceship. It was just the way he thought it would be. "Oh, this is so neat!" Steve said out loud. His voice still sounded like a mouse's voice.

A spaceman came through a little door. He took off his helmet, and Steve saw that he had fur all over, big ears, bright eyes, a long nose, and whiskers.

"Hey! You're a mouse!" Steve said.

"So are you," said the spacemouse. The spacemouse pointed to a mirror.

Steve looked in the mirror.

"Hey! I'm a mouse, too! How did I get to be a mouse?"

"You mean you weren't always a mouse?" the spacemouse asked.

"No! I was a human until a little while ago!"

"Well, you're a mouse now. You can believe me. I'm a mouse myself. I can tell."

"This is strange. I'm a mouse," Steve said.

"Do you mind being a mouse?" the spacemouse asked.

"I guess not," Steve said. "I like the whiskers."

"Everybody does. Were you the one hollering about the black hole a few minutes ago?"

"Yes," Steve said. "I was trying to warn you. There's one really close to us."

"We know that," the spacemouse said. "We're heading right for it."

"But won't it suck us up?" Steve asked.

"Of course it will," the spacemouse said. "That's what black holes do."

"But won't it squirt you into another world?"

"Yes! It's fun! We're about to go through it right now!"

"Right now?" Steve asked.

"Look out the window."

Steve looked out the window. "I can't see anything. It's all black."

"That's because we're going through the black hole," the spacemouse said. "We don't know where we'll wind up. Isn't this fun?"

"How am I going to get home?" Steve asked.

"Don't worry about it," the spacemouse said. "Be a brave spacemouse."

"What about the spacemen . . . I mean the spacemice I saw outside?" Steve asked.

"They've come in the back door. Don't worry so much," the spacemouse said. "By the way, my name is Roger."

"My name is Steve."

"Pleased to meet you," Roger said. "Would you like to go outside and see where we've landed?"

"We've landed?"

"So it seems." Roger began to open the door of the spaceship.

"I wonder what made me turn into a mouse," Steve said.

"No idea," Roger said. "Funny things happen in space."

6 Planet of the Bunnies

Outside the spaceship, most things were blue. The grass was blue, the trees were blue. There were big white bunnies grazing everywhere.

"You like bunnies?" Roger asked.

"I used to have them on my wallpaper," Steve said.

"Well, there's lots of bunnies here. Don't do anything to get them mad."

"Bunnies won't hurt you," Steve said.

"Just the same. Let's be careful," Roger said. "Look, here come the other mice."

Steve met the other spacemice. There were five of them.

"This is Steve," Roger said. "He doesn't know how he got to be a mouse."

The other spacemice thought that was funny. They gave squeaky mouse laughs.

"Well, let's get busy and explore around," Roger said.

"What are we looking for?" Steve asked.

"Gumballs would be best," Roger said.

Steve and the six spacemice, including Roger, walked around the blue world. The bunnies paid no attention to them.

"There's nothing here but grass and trees and bunnies," Steve said to Roger.

"There's a river!" Roger said.

The seven spacemice, including Steve, made their way to the side of the river Roger had seen.

"It's a river all right," Roger said.

"Here's a boat!" one of the spacemice shouted.

"Good! Let's get in and take a ride," Roger said.

"Wait!" Steve said. "This river seems to run very fast. How will we get back to the spaceship?"

"Don't worry about it," Roger said. "Be a brave explorer mouse."

The spacemice all got into the boat.

"There are only five paddles!" one of the spacemice said.

"Five will be enough," Roger said. "I will sit in the back and steer with my tail. Steve will stand in the front and look out for rocks. Louis will sit in the middle and sing. The rest will paddle."

The spacemouse explorers took their places. Roger wiggled his tail in the water to steer the boat, but it did not go very straight. Steve stood up in the front and kept a sharp lookout for rocks. The mouse named Louis sat in the middle and sang a song. The four other spacemouse explorers kept time to the song with their paddles. The paddles went "chunk, chunk," as they hit the water.

The song was about Steve.

He doesn't know...
(chunk, chunk)
how he got to be a mouse.
(chunk, chunk)
He doesn't know...
(chunk, chunk)
from where his whiskers came.

(chunk, chunk)

He doesn't know...
(chunk, chunk)
how he got to be a mouse.
(chunk, chunk)
And Steve...
(chunk, chunk)
Steve's his name.
Ooowee, ooowee!

All the mice joined in when they sang "Ooowee, ooowee."

7

Over the Falls

The boat was going fast. The spacemouse explorers paddled and sang, and the paddles chunked and the water sloshed against the sides. Steve liked being in the boat. It was as good as being in the spaceship. He felt like a brave spacemouse explorer, standing in the front and looking for rocks.

"Have you seen any rocks yet?" Roger called to Steve.

"Not yet," Steve said.

"If you see a rock, you let us know."

"I see a rock!" Steve shouted.

"Where is it? Point to it!" Roger shouted.

Steve pointed to a big rock.

Roger swished his tail in the water as hard as he could, and the boat skimmed by the rock, barely missing it.

"I see a lot of rocks!" Steve shouted. "And the river is getting narrow, and the banks are getting steep, and the water is going very fast!"

"It's the rapids! It's the rapids!" the spacemouse explorers shouted. "Hang on tight!"

It was impossible to miss the rocks. There were too many of them. Roger swished his tail left and right, but the boat banged and bumped against rocks, and turned and spun in the fast water. The spacemouse explorers and Steve were shaken and tossed. Steve could barely stand up, and had to hang on to the sides of the boat as tightly as he could.

"I don't see any more river!" Steve shouted. "It just sort of drops out of sight!"

"It's the waterfall! It's the waterfall!" the spacemouse explorers shouted. "We're going over. Ooowee, ooowee!"

Steve peeked over the front of the boat just in time to see nothing but a long drop ahead. "We're going over!" he shouted.

"Ooowee, ooowee!" the mice sang again.

The boat went crashing over the waterfall. The space-mouse explorers were thrown out of the boat and splashed and struggled in the water. It was scary. Everything moved very fast.

Steve didn't know what was happening. He couldn't see because of all the water splashing, and he couldn't hear because of all the water splashing. The next thing he knew he was crawling out of the water onto a big rock. The other mice were crawling out, too.

"That was exciting," Roger said. "I guess we'll just have to walk now. Maybe we'll find some gumballs soon."

"How are we going to get back now?" Steve asked.

"Don't worry about it," Roger said. "Right now, we'd better climb this mountain."

The spacemouse explorers had crawled out of the river at the foot of a mountain.

"That's a big mountain," Steve said.

"It sure is," Roger said. "Let's get started. Everybody take hold of the tail of the mouse in front. I will go first, and Steve will go last."

8 Mountain Mice

The spacemouse explorer mountaineers started up the mountain. Roger climbed at the front of the line, and Steve climbed at the end of the line. Louis was in the middle and he led the spacemouse explorer mountaineers in a song to keep up their spirits.

He was a kid...

Doowah, doowah.

Now he's a mouse...

Doowah, doowah.

He's looking for gumballs...

Doowah, doowah.

As big as a house...

Doowah, doowah.

As big...

Doowah.

Big as a house...

Big as a house, big as a house.

Doo Wah Doo Waaaaah.

26

As the spacemouse explorer mountaineers climbed higher and higher, the trees got smaller and the rocks got bigger. It got cold and colder, and the wind blew harder.

"Are we getting close to the top?" Steve shouted to Roger.

"I can see the top!" Roger called back. "It's got snow on it!"

Soon the seven spacemouse explorer mountaineers stood together on the peak.

"You mice did a beautiful job climbing this mountain," Roger said. "I've got cornflakes for everybody."

Roger pulled a crumpled bag out of his pockets, and poured some cornflakes into the cupped hands of each mouse. The seven tired but proud spacemouse explorer mountaineers sat on the top of the mountain, eating their cornflakes.

"Boy! You can see everything from here," Roger said.

He was right. They could see hills and valleys, and rivers, and other mountains and a little town.

Toboggan in Space

"See that town?" Roger asked. "That's where we should go."

"To look for gumballs?" Steve asked.

"That's right."

"How will we get down there?" Steve asked. "It's all snow on this side of the mountain."

"We'll slide down," Roger said. "We'll slide the whole way."

"It's miles!" Steve said. "We'll be going a million miles an hour by the time we get there!"

"Don't worry about it," Roger said. "OK, mice. Get ready to slide. Everybody sit down in a line and hold on to the shoulders of the mouse ahead of you. Steve will be first, and I will be last."

The first six of the spacemouse explorer mountaineer toboggan team sat down in a row, and Roger put his paws on the shoulders of the last mouse and pushed. As the line of mice moved forward, Roger sat down, holding on to the shoulders of the mouse ahead of him.

The line of mice swooshed down the slope. They went faster and faster.

"Isn't this nice?" Roger shouted to Steve.

"I'm scared!" Steve shouted back. "We're going too fast!"

"Don't worry about it!" Roger shouted.

"I want to slow down!" Steve shouted.

The mice began to sing:

He wants to slow down...
Doodoo doo doo.
Doodoo doo doo.
He thinks it's too fast...
Doodoo doo doo.
Doodoo doo doo.
But we're heading for town...
Doodoo doo doo.
Doodoo doo doo.
To find gumballs at last...
Doodoo doo doodoo doo
doodoo doo dooooo.

"It really is too fast!" Steve shouted.

Steve was right. The snow had started to get bumpy and the spacemouse explorer mountaineer toboggan team was bouncing up and down and rocking from side to side. Each bounce was higher than the last. The mice were having a hard time holding onto one another.

They hit a big bump and got disconnected. Now every mouse was rolling down the slope. Steve felt himself tumbling over and over. He could feel himself turning into a big snowball.

He heard the other mice shouting. "Yaaaay! Whee!"

Now there was a very very big bump. It was like a ski jump. Steve felt himself lifting high into the air. The other mice were shouting "**Gumballs! Gumballs!**"

Steve could just peek out of the ball of snow. He was rising into the sky. The sky was dark, with stars. He rose higher and higher. He didn't know where the rest of the spacemouse explorer mountaineer toboggan team snowball gumballs were. He went up and up.

Just when he thought he would go up forever, and never come down—he began to come down. Steve tumbled through the darkness, turning around and around.

He landed. Thump. He was in a big white snowfield. Over

his head was a night sky full of stars. The snow was not cold. It was smooth. It felt almost like a sheet. It felt just like a sheet. He could see spaceships glowing in the dark, all around him.

The next morning at breakfast, Steve's mother and father asked him how he had liked sleeping with the new wallpaper.

"It was fine," Steve said.

"You were able to get to sleep without any trouble?"

"No trouble at all."

"We were worried," Steve's mother said, "that you might be so excited that you'd have strange dreams."

"No, it was fine," Steve said.

"And you still like your spaceship wallpaper?"

"I like it better and better," Steve said.